T0104023

SOCIO JOURNEY

AM I A BOGOUR

SAMUEL R. WATKINS

 www.trafford.com

North America & international
toll-free: 1 888 232 4444 (USA & Canada)
fax: 812 355 4082

INTRODUCTION

THIS BOOK SOCIOLOGY – "what is or ought to be". We are aroused by sudden death of a young father. WE share and endue sympathy and grief with a young mother who assumes family responsibility. We are intrigued as the story unfolds revealing the tenacity for education and fervent maternal care.

With excitement, we join our friend Samoa on his journey, his first plane ride that takes him away from home in Africa to an unknown country, London England.

Samoa will be exposure to sociological conditions of various degree of stress.

The book describes situation and condition that causes distress and social characteristic. As we read we will understand why patterns of distress exist. We find sociological limitation that describe blacks have more distress than white due to long period of slavery.

DEDICATION

This book is dedicated to Mrs. Sadie Louise. Deshield, COUSIN for supportive and motivation to have and read this book.

Special thanks to my daughter, Rev. Mrs. Eddie-mae Abusmail for prayerful hours spent with us reminding that our heavenly father is in control. "Whatever will be will be."

Discussion with Samoa, this Cleaver alert and apt young boy, with interest to know the young boy, we ask about his family.

He apathetically explains, "My mother told me, my father died in a tragic accident a few days after I was born."

He further sympathetically explained,"MY mother is alone after the death of my father and she has responsibility to provide for us."

Samoa understands the situation his mother, a young woman is left alone to endure. His mother must assume full responsibility to provide for her family.

Imagine a young woman recently married with a young baby is shocked to be told that her young husband, her soul provider is dead in a fatal accident.

We are aroused by sudden death of a young father. We grieve to know the situation his mother must encounter.

We are aroused as the story unfolds revealing the tenacity of this young boy for education and fervent maternal care. We are moved with sympathy and joined in singing "Sweet Mother"

Sweet Mother, The things you do for me.

Mama; I will never forget you Oh!

Sweet Mother you are my all in all I'll never forget you.

With knowledge of such tregady.We recall that one of the

Core areas addressed by sociology are the study of social stratification, the inequities of income, power and prestige.

We are further reminded that sociology spring from humanistic empathy and concern as well as from Scholarly scientific curiosity. We conceive that this young boy is very ambitious and determined to achieve his desired education.

With express concern, he refers to an observed document that reveals, "Blacks are disproportionately poor". He interestingly refers to self determination, the ideology that is something of threat to Black scholars. Such reference includes racial that is found in obtaining education and acquiring employment.

These are self assertive and purport to base their assertion on an evaluation of the realities of Black world. A thin line exists between being pro Black and anti white.

This is intrinsically interesting as an African devil constructing the wonder mystical hanging bridge in space. Something more than scientific curiosity underscores our interest. We understand that racial differences, status and income are problem in human sociology. It is the inequality in misery that makes the other inequality meaningful.

.Samoa is aware that he must acquire his education and maintain social prestige. He is fervently aware that his mother is struggling to provide for him.

FOCUS AND DETERMINATION

This very studious and determined young boy with his mother's welfare as focus, he graduates from High school. He enters College with ambition and Determination he earns a scholarship to study abroad in London England.

Samoa is excited with mixed emotion to make his first trip to go out of Liberia away from his home.

He is particularly excited that he is to travel by airplane his first plane ride. He realizes that the flight from West Africa to London England is a long distance that could take almost a full day or more considering the time zone change.

Samoa friends are with him at the Airport awaiting his flight schedule announced to travel at midnight, but is delayed. After a long waiting He finally boards the plane after a long wait. He is already tired from the long waiting at the airfield, his flight is finally announced, and Samoa boards the plain, and settled down for his long ride. The excitement of being on the plane with such comfort, he soon falls asleep.

Samoa is suddenly awakened by the announcement: –

"We are in Heathrow Airport, London England. All passengers disembark!"

Samoa is shocked and confused to see other passengers leave the plane. Guarded by an angel He hurriedly gets off the plane and seemed lost. He did not know what to do. He stands in the middle of the airport surrounded with his load of three suitcases that is Loaded with foodstuff he perceived valuable to him in this strange cold environment. Samoa is now the spectacle of attraction. He is puzzled not knowing what to do or where to go.

ON AIRFIELD

Samoa a cleaver individual, now considers himself to be a "Bogus" who is defined in the dictionary as "Specious SHAM." In his colloquial language, "Bogor" is Ignorant- a false pretender". Samoa invites you to join him as he narrates this particular experience on his journey.

AT THE AIRPORT IN ENGLAND

Samoa says, "In my dilemma a gentleman come up to me and politely said, "Sir." Is anything wrong, can I help?" I am surprise that such a gentleman offered to help me. The gentleman asked me, "Do you need help? I immediately said, "Yes Sir". The gentleman followed by asking,

"Is anyone coming to meet you? I quickly said yes, but suddenly rebut, and said, "I mean no Sir". No one is to meet me."

The gentleman finally said "okay, "Where are you going?

I became more perplex because I did not know where I was going. I only knew that I was in England.

At this moment another polite gentleman, I assume to be an airport official reached me. He instantly volunteered to assist. He informed me with assurance that he would help me get a taxi to take me to London. I had no idea where I was neither did I know where London is. I was now worried realizing that the plane

Brought be me from Liberia for England. This man is telling me that the taxi will take me to London.

I tried to compose myself, and waited patiently while the gentleman called a taxi cab for me.

The taxicab driver came to me and took my suitcases and placed them in his taxi cab. I followed him to the taxicab. The taxicab driver is polite and said,

"Governor, where to."?

I immediately said, "London." The man said "Okay MIC" not knowing what that meant.

I am curious to find out. I later found out that it is a friendly expression similar to that used in his home country, Liberia to say, "Okay My friend."

The taxicab drove off for a relatively long drive from the Heathrow Airport in route bound for London. Again I was confused because I did

3

not have a definite destination. I was quite. The taxicab driver realized that I did not have a specific address destination. He listened and waited for me to give him an address in London.

The driver than said, "Sir, it is quite late and you need to rest." He assured me that he could take me to a place where I could rest for the night. At this point, I am distressed, practically lost in a strange country. I began to think, pondering my mind for alternate input. I agreed to go along with the suggestion to get a sleeping place. The taxicab pulled up at a building and stopped.

The Driver informed me, saying "Sir. This is Black Fryer". You can go in and find a sleeping place for the night."

I was already tired from the long plane flight from Africa, the confused destination of the plane landing at Heathrow and not London. I am now on an uncertain taxi ride, from the Airport to an uncertain destination, a building where I might find a place to sleep at this late hour 2:30 am.

I gladly entered the building to find out the possibility for a sleeping place for the night. To my greatest surprise, I observed that there were both men and Women lying on the floor sleeping. I ventured to go over to a small desk I saw in the corner of the room.

I had to be careful in placing my foot to avoid stepping on others. The situation is frightening and certainly frustrating. I immediately decided to return to the taxicab and told the driver, "I cannot make it in this place"

Realizing my helpless situation, I remembered a letter that was given to me by the Secretary of State of the Republic of Liberia that is to be delivered to the Liberia Legation in London. I excitedly reached into my pocket and pleasingly, I found the letter.

To my pleasing surprise, the letter had the full address of the Liberia Legation in London. I am very happy and excited to read the full address. I took the letter out of my pocket with anxiety to announce my discovery. With eager and anxiety, I excitedly reached out to the driver and show the letter to the taxi Driver, and excitedly I said,

"I think I have found a way out of my dilemma that might hopefully provide a better sleeping place than I observed at the Black Fryer building."

I appealingly request the taxicab driver to take me to the address we now found on the letter envelop. I had the feeling that the driver was becoming wary and somewhat fed up with my undecided actions. I apologetically requested that we go to the address we have on the letter. The driver was still Polite, and willing.

I believe that his presence with me is providential. He read the address and said, Sir. I believe that this office is closed at this time of the morning.

And the day is now Saturday. I told him, with firmness, "No matter what! I want you to take me to this address since it is the Liberia Legation.

We drove out for a few minutes and the Taxi cab driver finally located the address. I was very happy and anxiously excited when I read the poster that indicated the Legation of the Republic of Liberia. The driver drove into the yard of The Liberia Legation. Being excited and anxious, I hurriedly went up the few steps and reached the front door of the building. I had no doubt I saw a door button that could be a door bell. I anxiously pressed the button several times. I must have alarmed the people in the house. I waited for a few anxious minutes and finally the door cracked open but still lashed by a door chain. A lady enquired, "Who are you"?"

This time I was thinking fast and cleverly. I immediately, responded,

"I am a Liberian in need of help." I follow ed with the urgency; I have an urgent and important letter for the Minister Extraordinary Plenipotentiary from the State Department of Liberia. Hearing this, the lady opens the door and invited me in. She said It is late or early morning and the Minister is asleep.

At this point I had gained my composure and was determined to stay in this building no matter what the consequence, because it is the property of the Government of Liberia. I saw a seat near the door entrance into the hall way. I politely took a seat and asked the taxicab driver to please bring my suit cases in the house. The lady then realized that I was determined; she took the letter and Went up the stairs. She later returned and asked me to please wait. "The Minister will be down shortly to meet me".

The Taxi Driver was patiently waiting to receive his payment for the taxicab. I called the Driver to pay him for this taxi services and particularly his assistance.

Just then I saw a tall slender elderly gentleman dressed in a nightgown with a tassel nightcap on his head. This is indeed a novelty for me. I was reminded

Of the story I read as a child, "The Shoemaker and the Elf". My first time to see a real man dressed with the nightgown and the nightcap. The Minister official, Plenipotentiary representing the Republic of Liberia, greeted me politely. He apologize for the situation. He explained that this is a bad time to be in London.

All hotels are full with guest for the London Festival. He asked that I be a little patient while he makes a telephone call to locate accommodation for me. After the telephone call, he said I have a hotel for you, but it is for only for one night. I was satisfied. I thanked him, and said I do not mind, I will rest for only one night until tomorrow when I expect better arrangements will be made. He readily agreed and made the call. He then called the Driver of the taxicab to take me to the Strand Hotel in Piccadilly Circle. The driver repacked my suitcases in the taxicab and we drove off. I was more relaxed now. I had found someone who I could call on in the morning. The taxi cab pulled up in the driveway of the Hotel. It is a large building centrally located in the busy center of London. The glittering neon lights were dazzling. I was amazed with the excitement of Piccadilly Circus. When the taxicab pulled up at the hotel, a gentleman reached for the taxicab and opened the door and held it open until I got out. The man was well dressed in a full evening suit and a top (hat). I was somewhat reluctant to have him standing patiently and politely holding the taxicab door offering assistance while I step out of the taxicab. This gentleman, who I thought was some dignitary, escorted me into the hotel. He assisted with professional dignity Then he rushed back to assist the taxi driver with my bags. I registered for my hotel room. After the registration was completed, I paid the taxi driver and expressed my appreciation with a handsome tip. Or what we in Liberia would call a good dash. The driver seemed very pleased and he offered to come back in the morning just to find out if I would need his service. Another gentleman took me to the elevator and escorted me to the floor with the assigned room. The elevator ride is thrilling. This young gentleman made sure that all of my bags were safely secured in the room.

I was impressed with the professional performance and polite attitude. I later found out that the respectful young man, who assisted me, with my bags is the Bellboy and the elevator operator. It was he who took me up on the elevator with my bags, to my assigned room. I remember that he opened the door and he politely escorted me into the room and made sure that everything of mine was alright and correct. I was Indeed surprise to have such luxurious room. I was tired and very warily sleepy. After the bellboy left, I undressed and lied down for a long sleep. I fell asleep almost immediately.

I woke up early with the urge to pee. I was in a fix. I was really jammed and did not know what to do. I did not know where to go to ease myself. I looked around the room and found a small bucket or pale. I thought it was the slop bucket. I took hold of the small bucket near the table. Without further thoughts, I pee in the small bucket. Now that I have used the bucket, I am faced with the problem of disposing the pee. While I was thinking on what I could do to get rid of the urine or pee, I heard a knock at the room door. I was frightened because, I had already slept one night in the room. This is another day. I remembered that the Mister at the office told me that I had the room for only one night. I figured the Hotel people had come to take the room from me. Now I am faced with two problems. I had to get rid of the pee or urine in the bucket and the next to figure

What to do about a place to sleep if I have to leave this hotel room. Weighing the situation, I decided the best thing to do is to stay in the room and do not open the room door. Imagine I was placing myself in room confinement. Fortunately for me, whoever is knocking on the room door has decided to stop and probably left. I was relieved. Now, I resigned to remain in the room and keep my room locked and refuse to open the door for anyone.

It is now Sunday. I could not go to the Liberia Council because offices were closed. Nothing I could do but to stay put in the room. I settled down to read my Bible the 23rd Psalm. I became content with my situation. Without fear, looking around the room, I Saw a document on the table. Reading I found that it was the directory of the hotel with valuable information.

Reading the document, I found detailed information about the hotel room and available facilities. It indicated the toilet, the bathroom, trash basket I Gained courage to explore the room.

I saw a door and I ventured to enter. I turn the door knob and pushed it open. To my surprise, I saw a room fully equipped with towels, soap toilet paper, tooth paste and small tooth brush. I was certainly amazed to find these things in this room. I wondered how these things get in this room. Despite my concern, I was happy to find them.

I had just eaten the farina and Accra ground nuts and I was feeling the urge to use the toilet. Still exploring, I saw a sign that indicated, "PULL THE CHAIN" I tried the chain and pulled on it. I heard water running and pouring into the toilet bowl. Anew that if I use the toilet, I could get rid of the waste by pulling on the chain. I hurriedly took the small pail that I was calling bucket with the urine or pee-pee and I empted the pee-pee (urine) into the toilet bowl and pulled the chain. To

My Surprise and delight water rushed into the bowl and the urine disappeared. I carefully washed out the small pale or bucket and placed it back near the table where it was originally. After successfully disposing of the waste I heard another Knock at the room door. I was prepared to deal with the person knocking at the door. I asked, "Who is it"? The lady voice, Voice responded, "Maid service Sir. I am here to clean your room." She continued, "Sir, would you like for me to clean your room now or later?" I Replied, "You can come in now. I opened the door and a beautiful lady entered apologetically saying I am very sorry Sir. I came earlier but you were sleeping."

I can do it now if you desire. She also informed me that the room service came to inform you that you could have free breakfast. She assured me that the Sunday restaurant is still open for service. She continued, Sir if you desire, I could clean up While you have your lunch. I was still skeptical about the room situation. I told the

Cleaner lady, I will remain here in the room while you clean. I decided to take a comfortable seat and read a newspaper that was left at the door. Before doing that, I felt the urge to go to the toilet. I asked the lady if it is alright for me to use the bathroom toilet bowl. The young lady replied, "Oh yes Sir it is yours to use". I ate some Accra groundnuts and wrapped up the chaffs in scrap paper until I could find possible way to get rid of it.

I asked the cleaning lady, where I could I possibly get rid of this trash paper stuff? The cleaning lady said, "Please Sir. Gave it to me. I will put it right in the trash basket." She took the paper and placed it into the small bucket or trash basket that I called slop bucket.

I courageously walked into the bathroom. To ease myself on the bowl the lady showed me. I satisfied myself and had a good pass I had stored from almost two days of desire. After all of my discoveries and self education, I am satisfied that I do not have anything to fear. I could stay in the hotel room for another day which is Monday when all offices including the Liberia Council General will also are open. Reflecting on my situation, in England, I was convinced of my inability to cope with obvious national geographical separation. Distinguishing The Air port and the City. I was deeply moved to conceive that I had ignored the necessity to consult the few citizens who might have been in some way exposed to such culture Environment.

I was moved to consider my original African situation and environment. I reflected on the improvised facilities for taking a bath practically exposed out of doors. To urinating or peeing practically openly exposed. Using the WC, bathroom toilet I could not conceive that these facilities were available for daily need. I realize that such exposure for normal daily use. I decided that such information must be made available to other young people to know when they travel and encounter such different social culture. They will be aware that such facilities and utilities are made available in the house for convenience.

I was indeed embarrassed and ashamed, when the cleaning lady exposed these things and explained the necessity for having these facilities in the room just for my comfort and use. She also informed me that such facilities are normal domestic social facilities that people feel deeply personal about. More than that, it is the despair that identifies the social facts, as social problem.

Samoa invites you and all of us to continue the journey with him on his way to register and enroll in school. He is to travel by the train to a town out of London called Croydon.

On the train I met a gentleman who politely greeted me with a censuring smile.

He looked at me very strangely and apologetically, he said, "Excuse me young man." "Are you expecting a summer?"

I was surprise that he asked me such a question. "I main no harm he said, I only

Want to make you aware, "This is October mid winter."

I became conscious of my outfit. I had on a Light cream flexi pongee suit with a panama straw hat and white shoes. The only thing that placed me in the time period of the season is a short blue flight jacket.

The Gentleman smiled when he observed that I was Shivering and said, "I mean no harm son, but I think you need to get some warm clothing very soon." The gentleman made me conscious of my situation and aware that I am really a Bogus or Bogor in London England. I was shivering from the unfamiliar cold chill. All turned out for the better. I have I gained a gentleman friend. My gentleman, friend,. continued, to say "I see you are here for school"

He further said, "Before I leave you, I leave this advice with you." "While you are here, make sure you get the best out of whatever you study. Do not absorbs only the surface or the veneer." Make sure you get the real core substance." The train

Was to stop. The gentleman was preparing to get off the train at the stop. In his Preparation to leave the train, He politely takes off his winter coat and generously gave it to me. I was shocked and surprise when he said, "This is my stop I am leaving the train. He continues said, "I want you to keep warm my son, and remember what I said, "Make the best of your profession."The train stopped and my friend said good bye". I enthusiastically said thank you! And waved good bye as the train left. His gesture and generosity accompanied with his wise advice, will be remember and cherish always as my goal. "Get The Real Stuff, the CORE not VENEERS."

SOCIO - JOURNEY-PSYCOLOGICAL STRESS

In time, Samoa a college graduate is motivated to pursue African studies with concentration on sociological concept of the real world where Black people live. His involvement is research survey that meets the three criteria; Religion, job market and Socio-political affiliation.

Two things combine to produce psychological stress. One is the problem; the other is the inability to cope with the problem.

BLACK AND PRO WHITE

Foremost is the problem of human relations. The problem of Race, he noted to be the area of disadvantage. It is observed that in the United States blacks are disadvantaged and are disproportionately poor. On the average, blacks assumed to have lower level of education and less income than white mainly due to long history of discrimination.

Blacks have higher level of sociological stress than whites. Studies reveal that blacks encounter several aspects of discrimination including blocked opportunity. Such forms of segregations interfere with the upward mobility of the Black group due to discrimination. Blocked goals make a person feel helpless and powerless unable to control life. The picture is beginning to emerge and some obvious conclusions can be drawn. As is suggested, history can be both a methodical scholarly endeavor and Ideological force.

We must begin to place African history among the established legitimate history. Even though some African history seeks to affirm national cohesion and tend to portray the cultures of pre-colonial African states as harmonious and classless.

Africa has always been among the nations of the world from creation in vicinity of the Nile world in Africa. Research of Liberia in West Africa, reveals record of the first black group of Negroes free slaves of America. Some of them may have been those who left the home of their birth 1620 before the Civil War end slavery in the United States. Some of them may have been descendents of the very first African slaves landed in Jamestown, Virginia, USA in 1600 or earlier.

SYSTEM OF SERVITUDE

These first slaves were received under a system of servitude then prevailing which bound a laborer to his employer for a certain number of years after which he would be free. The condition of servitude was gradually restricted into permanent slavery.

Although some arrangements were adopted whereby a child of Negro slave, who's other parent was either white or Indian was considered free.

These Black slaves returned to the home country Africa 1824. They struggled persistently against many different groups from Europe and the United States including African seeking for wealth, exploiting Africa. In for wealth, exploiting Africa.

The only recognized Black group, The Republic Liberia persistently strived to abolish slavery and liberate Africa from the pre-colonial possession and slave trade.

We must search and seek answers to know the heights of African contribution to the progress of the world. This is a question which has trouble the world. Historian being mindful of the long European exploitation of Africa still deliberately denies evaluation of Africa's past,

The concept that infers and asserts that the continent below Sahara is only foot notes to the history.

Now that African studies have been present in major institutions particularly major American universities for more than thirty or more years and undertaken by dedicated scholars to study African contribution to the world that still remain undefined. Although the study of African history has burgeoned in the past several decades, it has shied away from any examination of the broader role of Africa in the world history, and contend itself with micro studies of discrete societies and migrations.

Western social scientist cleverly seeks to find such assumptions in early raciest statements that refer to Africa as DARK AFRICA.

African" History study is not to be understood as history of partial Africa, but the entire continent. Various forms of segregation has curtailed placement among the legitimate Branch of history.

MOVEMENT TO LIBERATE AFRICA

The intellectual conscious African scholars, seeking
Cohesion movement to liberate the masses from what they classify Europe-centric analysis and human degeneration to be able to produce alternative conclusion that combat the Western perspective of Black people.

This is significant challenge for Black educators responsible for completion of the work begun by students in early 1800 in Africa and the United States.

Imputing this can be met only by competent committed scholars who thoroughly understand the potential and power of Black representation and education as-Blaydon, Kanga history research, Richardson, Chassell, Watkins history etc.

This Chapter records the HISTORICAL events of Black achievement. It reveals the only effective Black African representative, Republic of Liberia. In 1920, actively affiliated with the League of Nations and the United Nations, of which they are Elected Members.

History, records the Republic of Liberia, the only African nation, representing the Black world. This Black representative, Liberia encountered the evil of colonialism and white supremacy who continued to conjure the phantom civilization of Ethiopia. This revelation reveals little or no information of civilization, but much of slave trade,without the steady state of Stone, age culture that had survived as long as 250,000 years. It went on to accuse Africa and dignified representative of enslaving their friends, wives and children.

AFRICAN STUDIES

This young scholar Samoa, On the Journey with devoted interest in African studies is motivated to compare his country Liberia in Africa with the other white environment that has in place segregation to keep the blacks out of the white environment.

He found out that the white group was more interested in occupying Africa and taking from Africa what they wanted to maintain and improve their Colonial selfish desires, particularly using the oppressed black to achieve their desire.

It is amazing that his concern is for young ambitious Africans to be able to travel to the United States of America the land of African slavery.

Black history is now relevant even indispensable. It has imposed a classification on the black population to compromise the undesirable segregation. Black is officially accepted as African American Instead of enforcing sectionalism or separatism that distinguishes BLACK and white. Black history is relevant. Black scholars include the critical understanding of the past and phenomena of the puzzles of Black life.

When there is a problem of race, their causes and explanations lay in the past. It is revealed that the period of Black history have been through many obstacles, serious challenges, great demands and expectations.

The achievement however is appreciated when nations of Black slavery changed to qualify the institution of Black world. They come together and initial the Conceptual parameters and explain the scholarly methods and purpose for what was generally referred to as Black studies.

CHANGE CAN DO SO MUCH

It is amazing that evolution and time can do so much. Scientific studies, has gradually changed the way of life and imposed different concept of human Appreciation and different attitude of relation within the world from the concept Of Black and white. Anthropology, scientific studies have imposed a more conducive human relation and more serious view of human relation that is more conducive considering theological declaration of creation and theory of evolution. That certainly broadens the outlook of humanitarian concept of the world.

Africa trade is more demanding with broader perspective of human relation. Neocolonialism and the pre-colonial era none existing. The world has major accepted changes.

Africa has made drastic adjustments with changes. The United States has encountered major political and social revolutionary changes in relation of black and white.

Before the fugitive Slave Law of 1850, runaway slaves escape to the free Northern States to begin new lives. Most fugitives had few job skills, could not read nor write. Segregation of all facilities doors closed to Blacks.

1920 -1940 United States experienced a major economic depression, attack on Perl Harbor, and the German alien invasion of North Africa initial World War II.

1943 President F.D. Roosevelt of The United States is visiting Liberia in West Africa. The question is asked, what is the most powerful and dominant allied

Leader of the world, doing in small tropic West Africa country while the world is consumed by war?

The answer is found in the special role LIBERIA played in the war effort during World War TWO. United State is specifically seeking partnership for a military base for US and British Military forces during the initial crises with Germany and Axis Japan in World War 11.

US is seeking assistance to obtain a suitable base for 5,000 Black African American troop to be stationed in Liberia West Africa to manage, store and maintain their military inventory at this military base. There was much debate of white and Black for control and use of the equipment. It is important to note that the Black African American troops who effectively stored and maintain the military

Inventory at Roberts Field in Liberia are the envious trained qualified US military pilots of Tuskegee. These Black Pilots are mindful of the existing feud of segregation; they are particularly mindful that the base is in Liberia the home of people of color. As such they refused to let white American troop and British Military fly supplies through Roberts Field, Liberia. The situation became so tense, that the matter had to be settled between President F.D. Roosevelt and PRIME Minister Winston Churchill at their meeting.

General Ike D. Eisenhower a renowned US General serving in North Africa with President Roosevelt admitted that he sincerely considered using LIBERIA in West Africa as the initial staging ground for(the inventory and as the initial staging ground for the invasion of North Africa and Europe.

He was convinced that Liberia's strategic location from Brazil and North Africa war zone was important. Liberia is the only country where the United States and Allied could obtain their supply of natural rubber.

Tending to unite people after World War TWO, the congenial slogan, of confidence "I got your back" is used. At the instant of the tragedy of Pearl Harbor.

And New York, terrorist attacked the World Trade Center in New York. The congenial slogan "I got your Back "is viewed by young Africans particularly the ambitious young scholars who dedicated their young life to achieve world unity and perpetuate African studies with concentration on Black African studies.

To better understand that, African Studies begins with Black History that it is relevant, even indispensible of other subject of Black history. Places them in perspective, establishes their origins and development, and thus aids critical discussion and understanding of them.

TIME CHANGE

The United States Government provides easy access to immigration facilities. Young African and others, take advantage of the available existing immigration

Facilities. NEW health education and travel guidance. They take advantage of the available financial opportunity. During the period on his journey, Samoa, a graduate is privileged to travel to the United States where he encountered another situation with segregation that motivated him to study Black African history.

Samoa the character of this story," Socio Journey" is motivated to study Black history with interest on movement of Africans after the abolition of slavery.

The Republic Liberia Samoa's home from where his journey began. He realizes that the world Perspective to human relation has change. The United States is progressively asserting better humanitarian and social progress between Black and White. Black population is officially recognized as African American and the American people are anxiously seeking scientific means DNA to determine the genetic and placement particularly to find who they are after such long period of slavery. The growing population is profoundly pleased considering the upsurge of mix population. Black students agitate for new relevancy, recall progressive act of the past. Men and women have engaged in critical estimation of American society

From the perspective of Black Americans. This is motivated when pioneers in African American history observed that the system of education in America conspired to teach Black people to despise themselves.

The times and human relation has changed. Liberians and Africans New immigrants are travelling with better knowledge of the social and cultural requirement. Samoa in this book put forth effort to enable Liberians who are refugees in 1980. They demonstrate and agitate for new relevancy.

BLACK STUDIES

This has existed in the past when men and women for many years engage in critiques of American society from the perspective of Black African.

We prefer to use the phrase, "African Studies" to that of "Black studies "Black is an honorable word with outburst change. We are glad to see many people now lose their fear, in using the word Black. Even-though It has limitations.

Black or Blackness; Tells us how we look without telling us who we are. While, Africa or "African" relates us to land territory, history and culture. No people are spiritually and culturally secured until it answered to a name of its own.

A name that instaneously relates to a people of the past, present and future as Liberian people. The name given by AFRICAN Free men, representing Freedom Liberty for people of color.

AFRICAN Studies reveals the past and the fate of Black people in America, the Western World. Particular reference –THE WILLIE LYNCH LETTER -self imposed brutal demonic inhume imposition invitation of the United States Congress psychology of the African slave trade. REVEALING insight of brutal and inhumane psychology and materialistic view point of southern plantations owners, revealing that slavery was a business victim of cattle slavery. Black were mare pawns in economic gains.

BUTCHERING, cross breathing, interracial rap and mental conditioning of the Negro race. The Negro is considered sub-human that influenced the slave trade. Within the time frame of African history relatively one and a half century 1712, Willie Lynch was invited by the United States Congress to help the colony of Virginia solve some of their problems with slaves.

WILLIE LYNCH LETTER- Present day with Stain- US CONGRESS invited satin with much controversy that ranges around the creation and intrusive meaning.

This is the most ancient story of the world. It has survived because it embodies the basic facts of human life. A fact that has not changed amid all the superficial changes of civilization. This fact remains the conflict between good and evil and fight between man and devil. The eternal struggle between human nature and against sin.

You will find the mind of man fed by the passion, hope and fears of new and strange earthly existence. In the zest of self expression, in the realms of mythology where swiftly the aspects of nature assume manifold personalities and the amorphous interest of sin takes on the grotesques of visible evil.

From such imaginative surroundings you find yourself starring at invisible events of self glorification and power. With the wicked satin who continue with no good with God, but thought he was created for naught and sought the God-head. But he was hurled down from heaven such is Willie Lynch. Lynch in the West Ideas on his plantation where he wickedly experimented with GODS' Creation some of the newest and still the oldest methods for controlling slaves.

Willie Lynch informs the U.S. Congress and people of Virginia, that he has the solution in his bags that work every time for controlling their black nigger slaves.

It is the interest and business of slave holder in particular with a view for practical economic results. Willie Lynch a worshiper of evil says let us make slaves. Not conceiving the power of God the only creator of man. Who in his divine authority said "Let us make man?" Lynch and others overlooking that the Divine Creator in love made man and breathed his breath into the image of dust of the ground.

SLAVERY- BREAKING

THE NIGGER being tied to the horse for orderly production. He focus on controlling the female male he called the savage. This motivated when a pioneer in African American history observed that the whole system of education in America conspires to teach Black people to despise themselves.

The idea is particularly referred to the characteristic of the white dominated education system wholly excluded Black in the history. Black people in America were defined by what White people taught them to be.

This turmoil's is its outward manifestation that Black studies begin with the study of Black history because it is reverent to all the other subjects' area of race. Black history places them in perspective, establishes their origin and development.

We prefer to use the phrase "African Studies "to the use of," Black Studies."".Black is an honorable word with outburst change. We are glad to see many people now lose their fear in using the word Black. It has its limitations. Black or Blackness. Whereas, Africa, or African relates to land and a Territory; history and culture. No people are spiritually and culturally secured until it answers to a name of its own. A name that spontaneously relate to a people of the past, present and future as "Liberian" People of the land belonging to a location in West Africa. Free people of color.

The topic Black Studies is inevitably representative of the writer. However this book of selected articles is reflective of continuing intellectual interest in the vital important task of assessing the intricate implication of the subject Black Studies. There is unique character and history in the development of Africa studies and history of Africa descent.

The development of African studies is indicative of the typical pattern generally associated with the modern Black movement, intellectual and social ferment. (Black Power rich interlace intellectual legacy based on the work of such people as Edwin Wilmot Blyden, Martin Delany Frances Harper and others.

SLAVERY THE NONE ECONOMIC GOOD OF THE NIGGER

African Studies is Indicative of the typical pattern generally associated with the concept of modern Black Studies. We trace the origin to the second Renaissance of the century during 1620 – 1900

based on the work of such people as Edwin Wilmot Blaydon, Martin Delany, Francis Harper and others. Liberia, the name given by African free men representing freedom Liberty and people of color.

BLACK STUDIES

This book of selected articles is reflective of continuing intellectual interest in assessing the intricate implication of the subject Black Studies which can be both scholarly and an ideological force.

It is the interaction of these two dimensions of historical consciousness which has led to the establishment of African Studies centers of Black American history.

it has become evident that the history of African people cannot be presented as conflict free, however grandiose such an achievement might have been.

Most African societies experienced domestic slavery and other form of oppression and exploitation. Their intensity should not be exaggerated.

It is necessary that we analyze the full range of African social organization and the process of internal differentiation which is evidence of reconstructing the History. We however, find the inequality of misery is a fact of everyday life to the extent that society is a creation of human action.

STRESS AND ATTRIBUTE

Why are some people more stressed than others? The answer is found in the reality of people's lives. Once we know the social patterns of distress we look for explanation.

The patterns suggest and reveal the social causes of psychological well being, Income and social classification...The probability of earning more than average income, or you are born white rather than Black.

AFRICAN STUDIES

Research study: Subscribe United States of America psychological deduction, political rival affiliations, Republican and Democratic. The logical indication is public contact and media release.

Psychological indication refers to the Republican background of slavery. Black and pro- white. It can possibly be conclude that the Political arena of racial distinction attributed to the Republican Party a probable cause by observing the regular media releases. Exemplified: "WE WILL BE FIGHTING THE DEMMOCRAT EVERY OPPORTUNITY."

Democratic Party obviously is enduring stress, but believes in party cooperation. Sympathizers are affected and stressful. The DNC Party should appease the public by redirecting attention to united national cooperation...

We summarize, synthesizes our observations and thoughts from a decade of research that reveal cause of distress for which psychology and psychiatry share differences.

From analysis of Pan Africanism and Islam we observe two alternative routes towards the African heritage: Africanism and Islamic,

These did first arrive in the Americas in chains. For it was brought to the Western hemisphere by West African slaves.

In reality the family under slavery was better able to preserve its African pride than to protect Islam identity.

Slavery damaged both the legacy of African culture and the legacy of Islam among the imported Black captives.

For a while Islam in the Diaspora was destroyed more completely than was Africanism now known as PAN- AFRICAN.

A contrast, indigenous African religion prospered more in the post Caribbean than in black America.

At that time Blaydon was already a professor of classic at Liberia College, West Africa...

While this idealization of simplicity can capture the minds after Blaydon, it seldom inspires the imagination of the African. The dominant North American culture is based on the premise of bigger better and more beautiful.

African American rebellion against Anglo-racism therefore seeks to prove that African has produce civilization in the past which were as big and beautiful than anything constructed by the white man.

AFRICAN

In the cultural atmosphere, African indigenous religion appears capable of being mistaking for primitive indigenous African rituals. Appear rural and village derived.

African religion does have an impressive following in part of the United States. The general predisposition of the African American paradigm of Nationalism is afraid of appearing to be primitive. =or Artisan

All of these options with particular reference to Islamic options are regarded by African American as worthier rival to the Christianity of the white man.

Major African concept seems to be an improvement upon the white man's Old Testament that once exercised Dominion and power over European.

Pan Africanism is conceived as alternative spiritual rote to the cultural bosom of the ancestral continent. Pan-Africanism is still the alternative route toward the African heritage.

AFRICAN CULTURE

After all, African culture first arrived in the Americas in CHAIN and it was brought to the Western hemisphere by African slaves. The family under slavery was better able to preserve its African pride and identity.

WILLIE LYNCH inhumane METHOD:

Controlling Slavery damaged both the legacy and African culture and spiritual beliefs among the important black captives.

With true independence regained, a new harmony is forged that will allow the combined presence of Africa and Euro Christian so that the presence is in tune with the original humanist principals underlining African society. Let us conclude with the role of Global Africa and how it has touched the lives of African thinkers, Edward Blaydon partly a linguist and philologist curious of the Arabic languish.

At that time, Blaydon was already professor of classics at Liberia College. To that extent Blyden was blazing a trail for Diaspora Africans.

AFRICA CONTRIBUTION

THE FIRST WORLD HEALTH ORGINATION 1952

1952 the first African meeting of the first Word Health Organization is held in Monrovia, Liberia. (1952).

In 1960 Liberia was the first African nation elected to the Security Council and her Ambassador Nathan Barnes presided over the Security Council during the critical period after the death of Secretary General Dag Hammarskjold.

The first American woman; The Second woman from any nation to be president of the UNITED Nations General Assembly was Liberia's Angie Brooks, who served on the Liberian delegation since 1953 That made her known as the outstanding woman diplomat at the (UN) UNITED NATIONS.

THE CONGO South African CENTERAL CRISES;

Liberia firmly backed United Nation peace keeping efforts.

Liberia made available A 245 –man Rifle Company the first to serve on foreign soil was sent to the Congo. Liberia sponsored a

Resolution opposing the resolution of the Casablanca block to put United Nation forces under African command.

Liberia was the first member nation to pay her share of the Congo peace-keeping operation.

Liberia has consistently sponsored and defended the cause of self determination and has taken lead at the UN in seeking Black interest

Liberia has played leading part in working for cooperation and harmony among African nations.

1959, President of Liberia, Tubman proposed the foundation of an associated state of Africa to consult on common problems and settle disputes and in 1960 advocated the pooling of African educational training resources in order to get maximum advantage and avoid costly duplication. The proposal by Tubman of Liberia was maintain.

1973 President W.V.S.Tubman of Liberia viewed Africa as community of states. Maintained that each state is to retain its own natural identity and that constitutional structure should prevail in the organization of African unity. This view was maintained into regional coordination. From which the Mano Union regional organization was formed.

1973 Liberia Sirraleon bounded by common factors of history agreed to establish the Mano River Union. The. Objective was to improve communication, unify their highway linking Liberia and Sierra Leone.

With thoughts and foresight, joint technical training facilities were undertaken in the technology of post and telecommunications.

Liberia provided managerial personnel.

The use of English as official language was an advantage.

In 1976 a new bridge was constructed between Sierra Leone and Liberia. Plans were made for agriculture and irrigation utilizing the Manor River BASIN which view is towards providing electric power sufficient to serve member countries, provide sufficient electrical power to extend to neighboring African countries.

Theme of the conference; "Decade of Transportation and Communication." Samuel R. Watkins of Liberia, submitted two documents "Staff Training" and "Africa must produce." To create demand for national material available for technical use in the technology of telecommunication and other technical utilities.

Recognized in social and behavioral sciences other than sociology, powerlessness appears in number of forms with various labels.

Liberia concern about unity and development in Africa became involved in the founding of the Organization of African Unity. OAU, now AU (African Unity). All these activities, lead to the PAN African Telecommunication technical integration.

The first chairman of the organization was Samuel R. Watkins of the Liberia Telecommunication Corporation. Mr. Watkins was elected president of the International Pan African Telecommunication within the ITU Technical Unite.

In this period the proclamation of the United Nation Transport and communication Decade for Africa was accepted. This was the historic decision for both UN and Africa. It was recognition by the international community that Africa's transport and communications were viewed from an integrated regional prospective a complimentary strategy of regional infrastructure development and integration across Africa.

1982 the first international Telecommunications conference, "The Monrovia conference" was held in Liberia.

It was important and significant that the first international activity of such magnitude be held at the period when the country is experiencing transition of government. The new government is not au-courante with the requirement for telecommunication and its international significance relation.

Sociological theory points to several likely conditions to produce a belief in external control.

The psychological inference of Powerlessness, accepted as objective conditions, Inability to achieve ones end's when they are in opposition to other. Structural inconsistency is a situation in which society defines certain goals purposes, and interest as legitimate and desirable.

(Many consequences including racism (and) against proposition (by the ability) to imagine a complex set of actions necessary to solve the practical problem Research 1979)

SOCIAL PATTERNS OF DISTRESS

That authoritarianism has many consequences including racism, judgments, and support for repressive and doctoral, practical explanation social patterns of distress. Two others are, particularly important in explaining social patterns of Distress. The emerging social paten of distress has the established omen of supra national, pan Africanism which has for long time been idealist aspiration for people of Africa and the African Diaspora.

BLACK STUDIES

WARNING ; possible interloping NEGITIVES

This creation of multiplicity of phenomena of illusions entails the principles of cross-breading the nigger and the horse to create a diversified division of labor Thereby creating different level of and different values of elusions.

History will forever remember the inhumanity of Willy Lynch against Negroes in the United States. We include the recorded

Stories of Negroes in the next chapter.

SLAVERY AND CONCIOUSNESS

AN OLD BLACK WOMAN STORY
EVIL OF SLAVERY

An 87 year old Black woman Laura Clark, near Livingston, SUMTER County, Alabama, born in North Carolina and bought to Alabama as a child tells, her story in her own understanding.

Said, "I been drug and put through the shackles so bad, I done forgot some of my children's names."

THE LIFE OF FREDRICK DOGLASS

An American slave tells his story. My mother and I were separated when I was just an infant. Before I knew her. As my mother. It is a common custom in the part of Maryland home from where I ran away to part children from their mother at a very early age frequently before the child has reached the twelfth month its mother is taken from it and hired on some farm considerable distant off and the child placed under the care of an old woman too old for field labor. For what purpose is this separation? I do not know; unless it is to hinder the development of the Childs affection toward his mother. To destroy the natural affection of the mother forms the child.

It is no surprise that greed and desire for power and control is still available wihen the Congress and government of the United States who invited the evil one, Willie Lynch to introduce his devised Demonic LETTER –his desire to assist in making a Slave by using Negro marriage UNIT:

It is no surprise that history record demonic Greed for power and control WILLIE LYNCH invited BY THE US CONGRESS to help control the slaves in Virginia.

Willy Lynch Letter.

HE began with breed two nigger males with two nigger females. Then we take the nigger males from them and keep them moving and working. Say the one nigger female bear a nigger female and the other bears a nigger male. Both nigger females, being without the influence of the male image Is Frozen with an independent psychology; will raise the offspring into reverse positions. The one with the female offspring will teach her to be like herself, independent and negotiable. –We negotiate with her, through her, by her and negotiate with her at her will. The one with the nigger male offspring, she being frozen with a subconscious fear for his life, will rase him to be mentally dependent and weal, but physically strong —in other words body over mind. Now in a few years when these two male offspring's become fertile for early reproduction, we will mate and breed them and continue the cycle. That is good, sound, and long range comprehensive planning.

LET'S MAKE A SLEVE for our control

PUBLISHED BY THE BLACK ARCADE LIBRATY -'

The God of our fathers who is always in control, dealt with Willie Lynch and all others who are part of such self acquired human power.

As God Almighty controlled the Devil-serpent, Adam and Eve, he also manifested his power Over The United States utilization of the deceptive Lynch Letter.

They are unaware that God is in control.

(He made Willie Lynch and others realize the power. When God breathed into the image of dust. Willie Lynch He informed those who attempted to control:

Gentleman, I did not come to solve your problems, you know what your problems are. I am here to enumerate your problems. However, I am here to introduce you to method of solving them.

It was the interest and business of slave holders to study human nature and the slave nature in particular, with a view to practical results. They had to deal not with earth, wood, and stone, but with men, and they by every regard they had for their safety and prosperity. They had needed to know the material on which they had to work. [Conscious of the injustice and wrong they were every hour perpetrating and knowing what they themselves would do were the victims of such wrongs are around... They were constantly looking for the first signs of dread retribution. They watched therefore, with skill and practiced eyes, and learned to read, with great accuracy the state of mind and heart of the slave, through his sable face. Unusual sobriety apparent abstraction, sullenness, and indifference in deed and mood out of the common way

Afforded ground for suspicion and inquiry. In common way the signs of dared retribution. They watched therefore with skilled

WE MUST NOT FORGET THAT THE African have keen and practiced eye. They learn to read with great accuracy the state of mind and the heart of the slave, through his sable face unusual sobriety apparent, sullenness and indifference in deed and in mood out of common way afforded ground for suspicion a hand injury, abstraction obtain astonishing proficient

Willie Lynch explains, "In my bag a is a foot long rope the method for controlling your Black slaves". I GURANTEE every one of you that if installed correctly, it will control your BLACK slaves for at least 300 hundred years. My method is simple; any member of the family or your overseer can use it.

I have outlined a number of differences among the slaves, and I take these differences and made them bigger. I USE FEAR, Distrust and Envy, for control purposes. These methods have worked on my modest plantation in the West Indies and it will work throughout the South. Take this simple little list of differences, and think THEM. On top of the list is AGE. It is there only because it starts with an "A" The second is color or HADE top of my list is "AGE" but it is there only because it starts with an "A" ; The Second is color or shades There IS intelligence, size sex, sex, size plantations, station on plantation size, plantation, station on plantation, attitude of owners, whether the slave lives in the valley, on the hill, east, west, north or south, have fine hair, course hair or is tall or short. Now that you have a list of differences I shall give you a line of actions. But before that I shall assure you that DISTRUST is stronger than TRUST, and envy is stronger than adulation, respect or admiration. Pampering bigger Niger for control purposes. These methods have worked on my modest plantation. I use fear distrust on my plantation in the West Indies and it will work for you throughout. Take THIS simple little differences and thinks of them. On top of my list is "Age", but it is there because on top

Of the list is "A" but A is there only because age starts with an "A" THINK THEM the South.

AM I A BOGOR

(Pan–Africanism and pan Islamism is still alternative routes toward the African heritage.

After all African culture first arrives in the Americas in chains- it was brought to the Western hemisphere by West African slaves. In reality the family under slavery was better able to preserve its African pride than to protect its other identity.

Slavery damaged both the legacy of American culture and legacy of African Gloria – true African religion.

Slavery damaged both their legacy of African culture and the legacy among the Black captives...

It remains to be seen whether the Twenty-first Century-with independence regain a new harmony to sustain harmony of Global Africa of tomorrow.

While this idealization of simplicity can capture the Caribbean mind both In this idealization of simplicity can capture the Caribbean mind both before and after Bl**yden IT INSPIRES THE IMAGINATION of the African American rebellion against Anglo racism before seeking**

To prove that Africa has civilization in the past which were as big and beautiful than anything constructed by the white man?

In the atmosphere of Gloria, the African indigoes religion is capable of being mistaken for primitive. (Its indigenous African ritual that appear real and village derived. While Global religion owing in part of the United States and rituals are often previously observed, in general predisposition of the African nationalism is afraid of appearing to be primitive. To sustain that the North American culture is based on the premise of bigger, better and more beautiful.

Africa.

Historians resolve to verify in discussion, confirms structural framework. Verified contention that no matter what happened to the Blacks during slavery, they always maintain a loving attitude. They highlighted the various activities of Blacks.

The Black African always aware of the creation and believe that God is love and cares for all his creation from the inanimate to his creatures.

As the creator in the Garden of Eden created Man father of all made it clear, when he informed Adam of his creation. He says, "satin was in heaven but because of greed and lust for power and control, he was cast out of heaven and hurled down to Earth and continue to deceive Holy creation in the Garden of Eden.

Willy Lynch and those of the Same, forget that it was the Divine Spirit

In his divine wisdom called the Divine Godhead and said, "Let us make man."

But Willie Lynch invited to associates in the US Congress, says,

LET'S MAKE A SLAVE. (Us congress –invites)

WILLIE lynch asked in congress,

THE ORIGIN AND DEVELPOPMENT OF A SOCIAL BEIGN-THE NEGRO

THE Willie Lynch, says what do I need?

First of all we need a black nigger man, a pregnant nigger woman and her baby nigger boy. Second I will use the same basic principle that we use in the breaking a horse, combined with some more sustaining factors.

When we do it with horses we bread them from one form of life to another, that is, we reduce them from natural state in nature; whereas nature provides them with the natural capacity to take of their needs and the needs of their offspring, we brake that natural string of independence from them and thereby create a dependency state so that we may be able to get them useful production for our business and pleasure.

CARDINAL PRINCIPALES FOR MAKING AND BRAKING NEGRO

--For fear that our future generations may not understand the------- --------- principles of breaking both horse and man, we lay down the art. For, if we are to sustain our basic economy we must brake and tie both of the beasts together, the nigger and horse. We understand that short range planning in economics results in periodic economic chaos, so that, to avoid turmoil in the economy, it requires us to have depth in longer range in loge range comprehensive planning, articulating both skill and sharp perception.

We lay down the following principles for long range comprehensive economic planning.

Attention must be crossbred to produce a variety and division

1) Both horse and nigger are no good to the economy in the wild or natural state

25) **Both must be taught to respond to a particular new language.**) Both must be broken and tied together for orderly production.

3) for the wordily future, special and particular attention must be paid to the female and the young offspring

4) Both must be crossbred to produce a variety and division of labor.

6) Psychological and physical instruction of containment must be created for both.

We hold the above six cardinal principles as truce to be self-evident, based on the following discourse concerning the economics of breaking slaves and inhumanely tying the horse and the nigger together-all inclusive of the six principles laid down above.

NOTE: Neither principle alone will suffice for the good economics. All principles must be employed for the orderly good of the nation.

THE CONDITION THAT IN THE 1970 HAVE PROCEEEDED

Over the past year there have been concern with numerous attacks

Over the past years there have been numerous attacks on Black studies. Some believe that a decade the system is ready to eliminate these. unites

(THE PROCESS OF EDUCATION ALWAYS BEEN EXTREME INPORTANCE IN America society. The methods if education the child is empowered as important.

Pan –Africanism and pan Islamism are still two alternative routes toward the African heritage. After all Islam's first arrive in the Americas in Chains- for it was brought to the Western hemisphere by West African slaves. In reality the family under slavery was better able to preserve its African pride than to protect its Islamic identity. Slavery damaged both the legacy of American culture and legacy of Islam.

Slavery damaged both their legacy of African culture and legacy of Islam among the imported Black captives. Of African culture and the legacy amount the Black captives... But for quite a while Islam in the Diaspora was restored. More completely. But mow

FRICAN negation in North America is perceived as alternative spiritual routes to the cultural bosom of the ancestral continent. it remains to be seen whether the Twenty-first Century- will see a similar equilibrium in the Blyden's Caribbean as the search continues for more authentic cultural and spiritual paradigms to sustain the Global Africa of tomorrow

IT REMAINS to be seen that whether the twenty first century

WITH THIS independence regained; a New Harmony need to be forged. A harmony that will allow the presence of Afro centricity.

Biblical import at the creation, the divine however informed Adam after the trespass of Eve. Research exposes the mind of men fed with passion hopes, fears of new and strange earthly desire.

The zest of expression, you roam in the realms mythology where swiftly the aspects of nature assume manifold personalities. Amorphous shapeless not crystallized, takes on the grotesqueries visible evils. From such imaginative conception, we find ourselves suddenly staring at commonplace family life such as the first family imaginative surroundings. This is the greatest discovery the world has known. It affects contemporary thoughts in molding judgment of the future generations.

The saint's angel was with God the Father, but greed and desire for power, aroused the Holy displeasure of our Heavenly Father and was hurled from Heaven in the Garden.

You have been enlightened with hope and love. You have absorbed the intricate substance of the gift of God our creator. WE must not forget that God with divine power, "In the beginning, "God with love created the Heaven and the earth. Biblical revelation reminds us that "God Is Love" We find in the holy book, that in the beginning God SPOKE THREE Words, LET THERE BE"........ and there was.

After all the atrocities of life, the spiteful encroachment deceptive inducement for power in various parts of the world, particularly Africa deceptive inducement and Slavery, We consider creation.

This is the most ancient story of the world. It has survived because it embodies the basic facts of human life. A fact that has not changed amid the superficial changes of civilization. This fact remains between good and evil and fights between man and devil. Good and evil, eternal struggle of human nature against sin.

You will find the mind of man, fed by the passion, hopes fears of new and strange earthly existence. In the zest of self expression in the realms of mythology where swiftly the aspects of nature assume manifold personalities and the aphorism intent of sin takes on the grotesques of visible evil, from such imaginative surroundings, you find yourself suddenly staring at unvarnished events of self glorification and power with wicked satin who continues with no good With God but thought that he was created for naught and sought the god head and was hurled down from heaven. Such as the Willie Lynch and others with him. He tried to substitute the creator and forgot the divine who said "Let Us make man. With Love breathed his grace of love into the image and man became a living soul.

EBOLA virus most deadly even in Africa, crises In the 2014

END STORY F S N &&&&&&&&&

END

Sweet mother
I will never forget you,
The things you do for me,
Your love and prayer,
Will linger always in my heart;
Sweet mother you are my all in all:
I will never, no never forget you oh!

Printed in the United States
By Bookmasters